The TORTILLA FACTORY

The
TORTILLA
FACTORY

Gary Paulsen

PAINTINGS BY

Ruth Wright Paulsen

Voyager Books
Harcourt Brace & Company
SAN DIEGO   NEW YORK   LONDON

First Voyager books edition 1998
Voyager Books is a registered trademark of Harcourt Brace & Company.

Library of Congress Cataloging-in-Publication Data
Paulsen, Gary
The tortilla factory/by Gary Paulsen; illustrated by
Ruth Wright Paulsen—1st ed.
p.   cm.
"Voyager Books."
ISBN 0-15-292876-6
ISBN 0-15-201698-8 pb
1. Tortillas—Juvenile literature. [1. Tortillas.]
I. Paulsen, Ruth Wright, ill. II. Title.
TX770.T65P38   1995
641.8'2—dc20 93-48590

PRINTED IN SINGAPORE

F H J L N M K I G E

…Through Your goodness we have this bread to offer,
Which earth has given and human hands have made.
It will become for us the bread of life.

—*The Sacramentary of the Roman Missal*

THE BLACK EARTH sleeps in winter.

But in the spring the black earth
is worked by brown hands

that plant yellow seeds,

which become green plants rustling in soft wind

and make golden corn to dry in
hot sun and be ground into flour

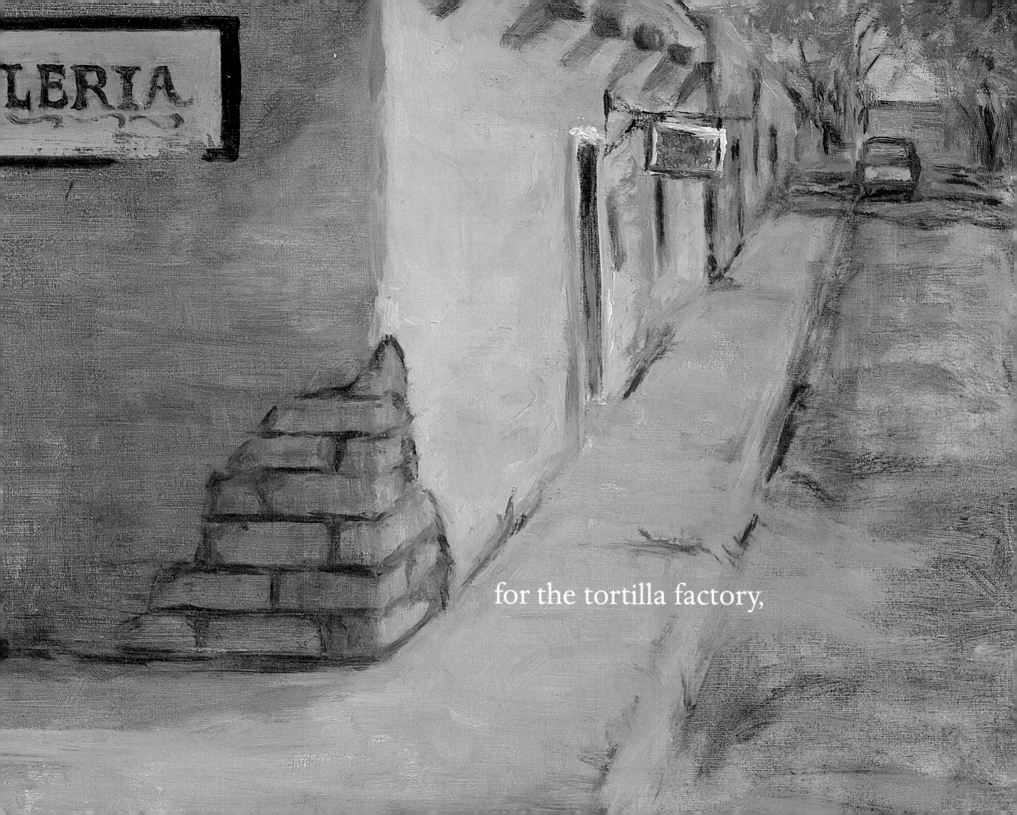

for the tortilla factory,

where laughing people and clank-clunking
machinery mix the flour into dough,

and push the dough,
and squeeze the dough,
and flatten the dough…

…and bake the dough into perfect disks that
come off the machine and into a package
and onto a truck and into a kitchen

to be wrapped around juicy beans

and eaten by white teeth, to fill a round stomach

and give strength to the brown hands
that work the black earth

to plant yellow seeds,

which make golden corn to be dried
in hot sun and be ground into flour....

641.8
PAU
Paulsen, Gary
The tortilla factory

36218

DATE DUE
